Weekly Reader Children's Book Club presents

Runaway Marie Louise

by Natalie Savage Carlson
pictures by Jose Aruego & Ariane Dewey

CHARLES SCRIBNER'S SONS · NEW YORK

Text copyright © 1977 Natalie Savage Carlson
Illustrations copyright © 1977 Jose Aruego and Ariane Dewey

Library of Congress Cataloging in Publication Data
Carlson, Natalie Savage.
Runaway Marie Louise.
SUMMARY: Marie Louise, the brown mongoose, runs away
after her mother spanks her for being naughty.
[1. Runaways—Fiction. 2. Mongooses—Fiction]
I. Aruego, Jose. II. Dewey, Ariane. III. Title.
PZ7.C2167Ru   [E]   77-9448
ISBN 0-684-15045-X

For
my little friends,
Megan and Guy Harrington

Marie Louise was a little brown mongoose.
She lived with her mama in a thatched hut in a field
of sugarcane.

She was usually a good little mongoose. But one day she
was naughty.

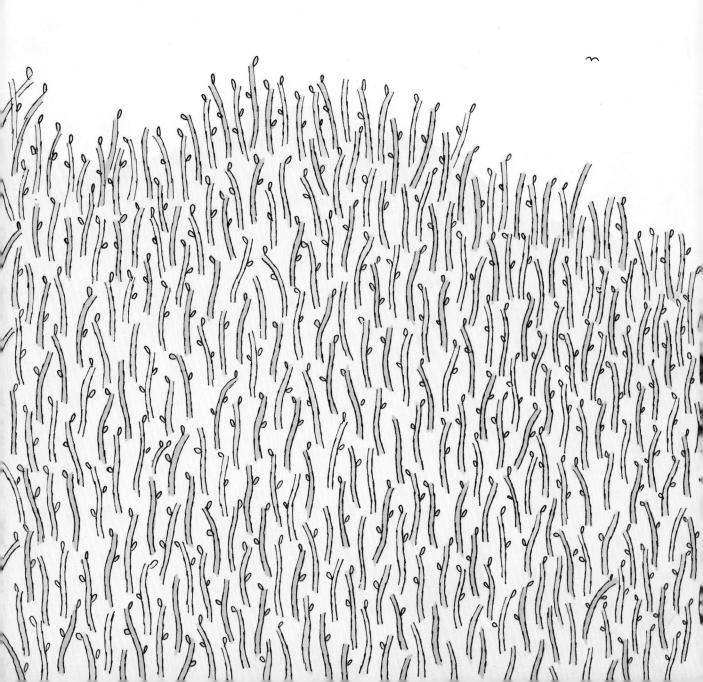

She cooked mud pies on the stove and they boiled over.

She cut a hole in her coverlet so her tail could hang out at night.

She and her little snake friend Christophe put a
buzzard's egg in an owl's nest.

So Marie Louise's mama gave her a spanking.
Marie Louise was mad at her mama. She put her
seashells in a sack and started for the door.

"Where are you going?" said her mama. "It is almost
time for lunch."

"I am running away," said Marie Louise. "You don't love
me anymore. I am going to find a new mama."

Her mama said, "It may not be easy to find a new mama. It may take a long time. You will get hungry. I will make a sandwich for you to take."

Marie Louise's mama made her a peanut butter and jellyfish sandwich. Marie Louise tossed it in the sack with her seashells.

First she went to Christophe's cave home in the rock pile.

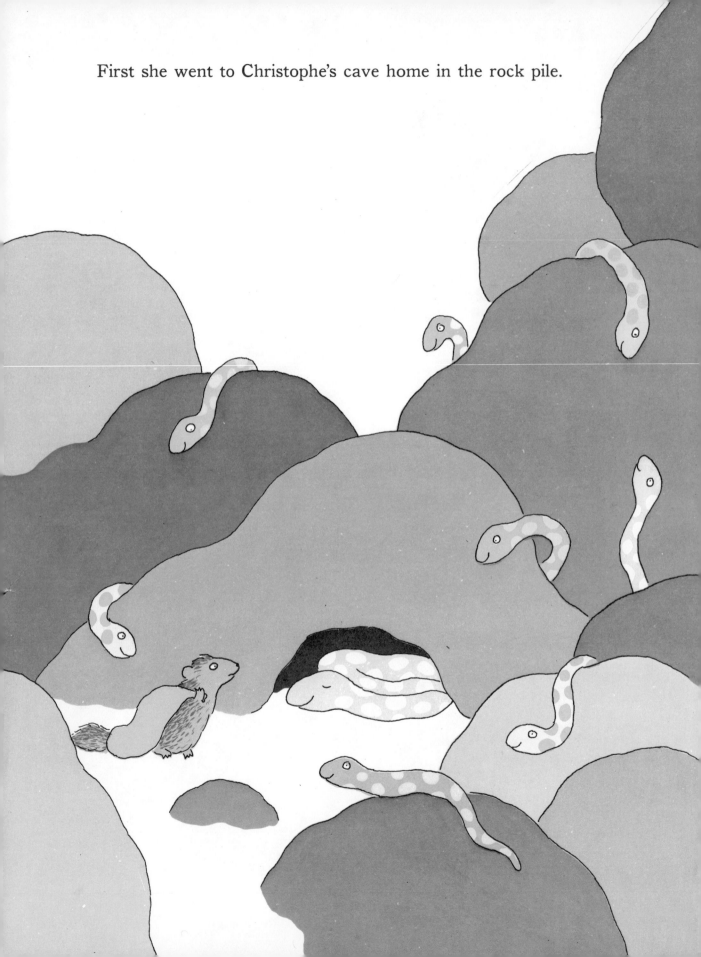

She said to his mama, "Would you like to have me for your child too? My mama doesn't love me anymore."

Christophe's mama said, "One naughty child in my family is enough. Another would give me the tail tizzies."

So Marie Louise went on to the boggy, soggy swamp.
She saw the Dabble Duck teaching her ducklings to
dibble for duckweed.

"Do you want another child?" said Marie Louise. "My
mama doesn't love me anymore."

The Dabble Duck twitched her tail and clicked her beak.
"No, no, and another no!" she said. "Can't you see I
have my beak full with these ten children?"

Marie Louise went on until she came to the fishy, swishy creek where the Snapping Turtle had parked her camper. She knocked on the back door, and the Turtle's tail popped out. So she went around and knocked on the front door, and the Turtle's head popped out.

Marie Louise said, "Can I be your child? My mama
doesn't love me anymore."

"Mud puddles and fishbones!" exclaimed the Snapping
Turtle. "I can't be bothered with children. I have laid my
eggs in a hole near here. When they hatch, my children
will have to care for themselves."

She pulled her head in and slammed the door.

Marie Louise went on until she saw the Banded
Armadillo digging in a squirmy, wormy spot. She jerked
the Armadillo's horny tail twice.

The Banded Armadillo stopped digging and turned
around.

Marie Louise said, "Do you want me for your child? My mama doesn't love me anymore."

The Banded Armadillo looked her up and down and sideways.

She said, "Ugh! Why would I want an ugly child all covered with hair? My own beautiful children would be ashamed of you."

Marie Louise was discouraged.

She said to herself, "Perhaps I should look for a papa instead of a mama. It might be easier to find one. I will go to the Witch Toad. He has no children so he might want me. I can learn magic from him and be a Witch Mongoose."

This idea pleased her the most.

She said to herself, "Then I can change mud pies into banana cream pies and buzzard's eggs into baby owls. I can make my tail disappear at night so it won't tickle me in bed."

Marie Louise climbed the hill to the big black rock where the Witch Toad lived. He was stirring something green in a big black pot.

Marie Louise said, "Witch Toad, do you want me for your witch child? My mama doesn't love me anymore."

The Witch Toad stopped stirring.

He said, "Can you cure hiccoughs and heebie-jeebies? Can you change monkeys into mice?"

"No," said Marie Louise, "but you can teach me."

"Runaways learn their lessons too slowly," said the Witch Toad, "so I don't want you."

Marie Louise hung her head.

Then she said, "Will you look into your magic ball and tell me where I can find a mama or papa?"

The Witch Toad said, "I don't have to look in my magic ball. A nice lady came here asking me to find a child for her. She just left by the jippi-jappa path. You may catch her if you hurry. But first, where is my pay for telling you this?"

Marie Louise quickly pulled her sandwich from the sack. She said, "I am hungry myself. But I'll give you this peanut butter and jellyfish sandwich."

Then she ran down the path so fast that lightning couldn't have hit her if it struck three times. She was in a big hurry to catch her new mama.

She hoped it wasn't Christophe's mama. She wouldn't
want to give her best friend's mama the tail tizzies.

She hoped it wasn't the Dabble Duck who had decided
that one more child didn't matter. Marie Louise would
have to swim and dibble all day long.

She hoped it wasn't the Snapping Turtle who now
wanted a bothersome child instead of eggs that took
care of themselves. There wouldn't be room for Marie
Louise in the Turtle's camper. She would have to live
outside in the wind and rain.

She hoped it wasn't the Banded Armadillo who had
decided she was beautiful after all. Marie Louise would
have to dig in the dirt all day with brothers and sisters
without any hair.

When Marie Louise reached the jippi-jappa trees, she saw her own mama's tail ahead. She ran faster and faster. "Mama! Mama!" she cried. "Wait for me. Where are you going?"

Her mama stopped. She turned around and hugged
Marie Louise.

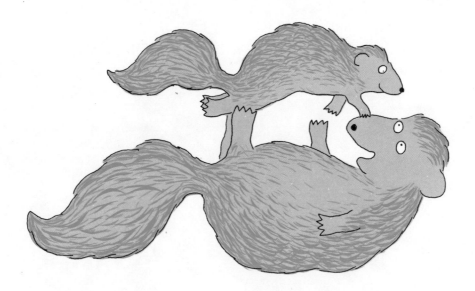

She said, "I am running away too. It would be lonely at home with no one to love and care for. Now where shall we run away to? Where is the best place?"

Marie Louise said, "You are really the best mama. Let's run away home. I think that is the best place."

"So do I," said her mama. "And when we get there, I will make a fluffy, puffy omelet."

So they both ran away to the thatched hut in the field
of sugarcane.